TRANSFORMERS RESCUE BOTS

Attack of the Movie Monsters!

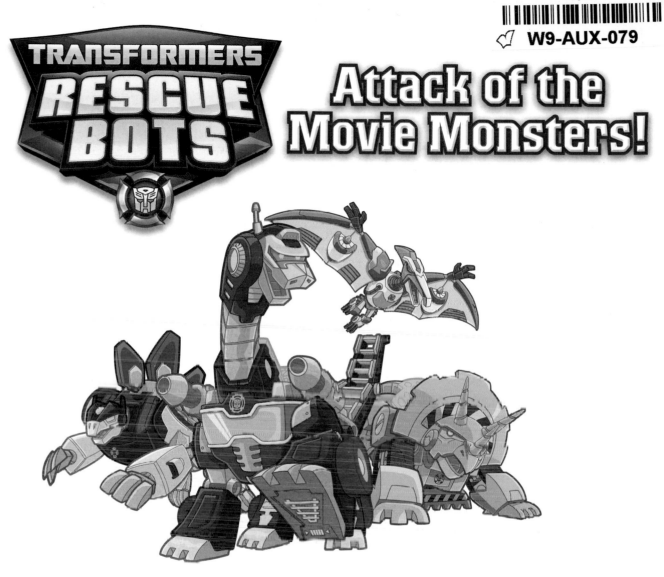

Adapted by Brandon T. Snider
Based on the episode "The Attack of Humungado"
written by Shannon McKain and Jackson Grant

LITTLE, BROWN & COMPANY
LB kids

Little, Brown and Company

Hachette Book Group
1290 Avenue of the Americas, New York, NY 10104
Visit us at lb-kids.com

LB kids is an imprint of Little, Brown and Company.
The LB kids name and logo are trademarks of Hachette Book Group, Inc.

The publisher is not responsible for websites (or their content) that are not owned by the publisher.

First Edition: October 2015

ISBN 978-0-316-30171-8

10 9 8 7 6 5 4 3 2 1

CW

Printed in the United States of America

Licensed By:

The Burns family and the Rescue Bots decide to see a movie at the drive-in. "Why do we have to watch some silly monster movie?" grumbles Dani.

"*Attack of the Humungado* is not just *any* silly monster movie," says Kade. "It's a *kaiju* classic!"

"And there's nothing better than movie popcorn!" says Cody.

Blades is unimpressed by the old film. "Look at how fake those monsters look. I've cleaned scarier stuff off my windshield," he says.

Suddenly, a terrible fire breaks out in the projection booth! Mr. Bunty, the projectionist, is in trouble. Chief Burns spots the flames from the hill and calls the Rescue Bots to action.

Chase helps guide the movie patrons to safety while Kade and Heatwave save Mr. Bunty. Blades uses his scoop claw to drop a load of water on the blazing projection booth, but it is burned to a crisp. The Rescue Bots promise to help Mr. Bunty any way they can.

The following day, the Rescue Team helps rebuild the building. Heatwave, Chase, Boulder, and Blades put the finishing touches on the projection booth by fixing the roof in place. Mr. Bunty is grateful for the team's kindness.

"Thank you! It's never looked better. I wish I could say the same for my projector," Mr. Bunty says.

Luckily, Doc Greene has a brand-new device for Mr. Bunty. "This is a Holomorphic Projector," explains Doc Greene. "It turns a two-dimensional movie into a hologram!"

"So the monsters can stomp around in the audience?" asks Cody.

"Indeed. They'll look more lifelike than you could ever imagine," says Doc Greene.

At the drive-in the next night, Kade and Mr. Bunty watch another *kaiju* movie, starring the monster Rayvenous. As Rayvenous appears on the screen, a power surge occurs, causing the projector to malfunction. Kade and Mr. Bunty don't notice that Rayvenous has actually come right out of the movie and into Griffin Rock!

The following day, Chief Burns gets a strange call. A monster is munching on the mayor's mansion. It is time to call the Bots.

"Rescue Bots, roll to the rescue!" says Heatwave.

They arrive on the scene to find Rayvenous feasting on the mayor's home. "It must have something to do with Doc's projector!" says Graham.

When Rayvenous dive-bombs the team, Heatwave blasts him with his water jets. The Rescue Bots shield their teammates as Rayvenous crashes into a fountain. The monster lets out a loud screech and flies into an underground tunnel to escape.

"As if it couldn't get any creepier," Blades says.

The Rescue Bots find Rayvenous snarling in a corner of the cavern. He attacks the Bots and starts chomping on Blades.

"Why me? There are others in the room, you know," says Blades.

Heatwave steps in to save Blades, and the Bots trap Rayvenous. They take him back to the drive-in for observation.

Doc Greene performs tests to determine what happened. He concludes that the power surge turned the hologram of Rayvenous into a solid creature with a taste for destruction. Doc re-creates the power surge, hoping to return Rayvenous to his previous state, but instead he brings forth a scary new menace: HUMUNGADO!

Humungado blasts his fire breath high into the sky and uses his massive tail to crush the Holomorphic Projector. Then he turns his attention to Rayvenous, who tries to zap him with ice. Heatwave and Chase grab Humungado's arms, and Boulder grabs his tail. The Rescue Bots aren't giving up without a fight.

Blades tries to stop the monster, but it's no use. Humungado lets out a loud roar and heads downtown.

"Doc, we're going after Humungado. Keep an eye on Rayvenous," says Chief Burns.

"Will do! I'll also work on fixing the projector," says Doc Greene.

The chief and Chase watch as Humungado rampages through the city. Blades tries to distract Humungado, but it doesn't work. Nothing seems to be working. Is Humungado unstoppable?

It is time for Kade, Heatwave, Graham, and Boulder to try their luck. They grab a gigantic steel beam, hoping to trip Humungado as he walks by.

"Hey, Humungado! Have a good *trip*. See you next *fall*," jokes Kade.

The monster snaps the steel beam like a toothpick.

"I guess he doesn't share your sense of humor," says Heatwave.

Humungado spots a billboard for the museum's dinosaur exhibit. It features a Tyrannosaurus rex. This makes Humungado *very* angry. He lets out another heart-stopping screech and angrily knocks over the billboard. Then he burns it to ash.

"Whoa! He must *really* hate dinosaurs," says Cody. "Or billboards."

"He hates *dinosaurs*. Everybody knows that. It's from the sequel, where Humungado and Rayvenous team up to fight Supersaurus," says Kade.

That gives Cody an idea. "Kade, you're a genius! If the Bots turn Dino, maybe Humungado will go after *them* and not the town!" he says.

"Rescue Bots, would you mind going prehistoric?" asks Chief Burns.

"You heard him. The Dino Bots are back in town!" says Heatwave. The Rescue Bots change into their dinosaur modes as Humungado attacks them with a fireball.

Heatwave neutralizes the fireball with a burst of water.

Boulder uses his seismic stomp to shake Humungado to his core.

Blades hits him with his sonic scream. Now Humungado is on the run.

Humungado comes upon a four-way intersection, but Chase is ready for him and blocks Humungado's path with his electrified tail. Humungado takes off toward the beach.

"It's working!" says Boulder. The rest of the Dino Bots follow Humungado to the ocean and corner him. The monster is now furious.

Blades uses the caged Rayvenous to lure Humungado back to the drive-in. Humungado is on the move again, letting out fiery belches along the way. A blast of fire hits Blades and sends him to the ground.

Now Rayvenous is free. Rayvenous and Humungado both hate dinosaurs and are going to join forces to destroy the Rescue Team!

Doc Greene is ready to use his Holomorphic Projector to send the monsters back into their movie world.

"We only have one shot at this. We need both creatures inside the holographic field in order for this to work," says Doc.

The Rescue Bots struggle to contain Humungado and Rayvenous. The Bots charge at them with everything they have and force the two creatures into the holographic field.

Doc Greene flips a switch that activates a power surge, which creates a huge blast of light. Then he turns on the lens of the projector. Humungado and Rayvenous are sucked back into the film. Griffin Rock is safe again, thanks to the Rescue Team.

"Now *that's* what the sequel should have looked like!" says Kade.

The next night, everyone settles down at the drive-in to finish watching *Attack of the Humungado* and all its sequels, upon Kade's request.

"Thanks, guys. It means a lot more with all of you here," says Kade.

Cody smiles. "That's what family does."

"Even if these movies are terrible," says Dani.

"Pass the popcorn?" askes Graham as Humungado roars safely on the screen.